HIDE & SEEK | MELBOURNE
HIT THE STREETS

GW00706043

CONTENTS

006 / LET'S GET PHYSICAL

026 / CULTURE CLUB

054 / LET'S GO OUTSIDE

066 / MIXED BAG

084 / RELAX MAX

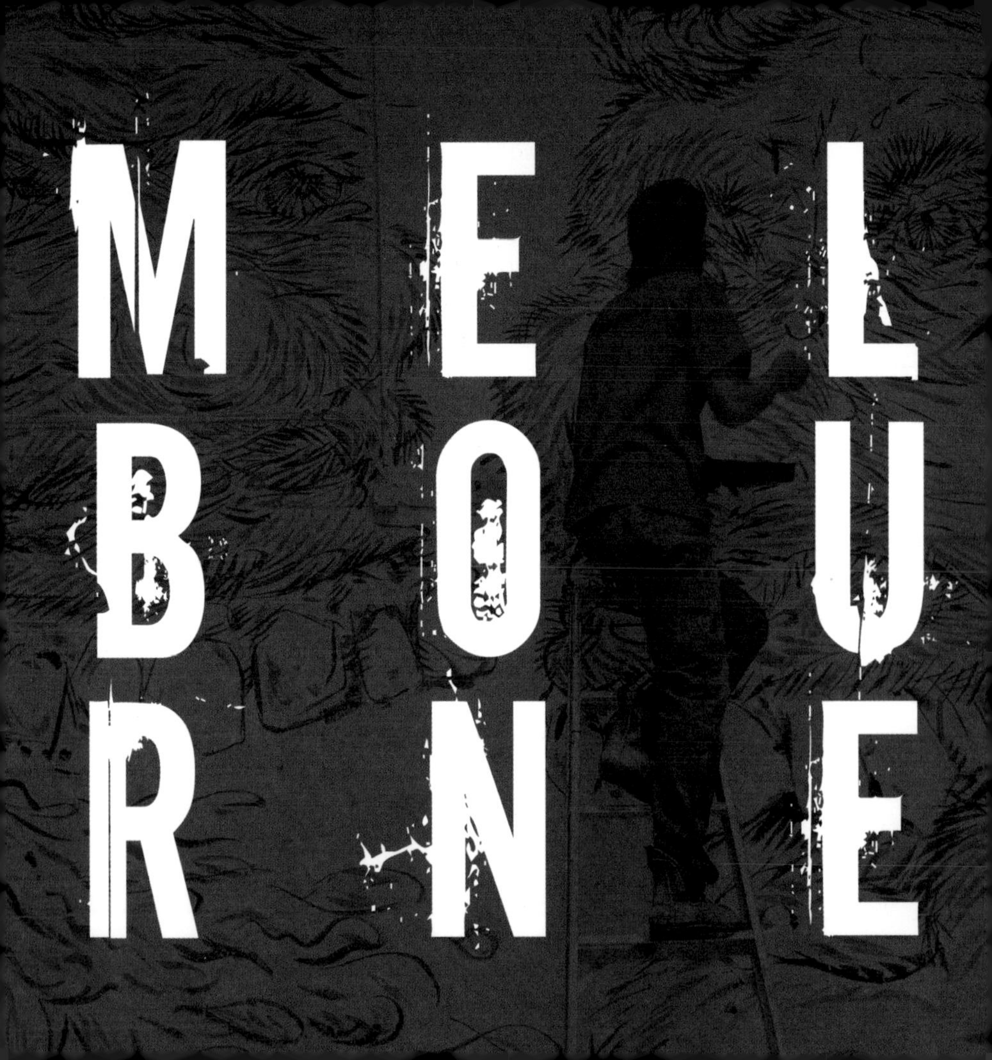
M E L
B O U
R N E

READY-SET-GO | HIT THE STREETS

When you're not sure what present to get for the friend/partner/sibling/parent that has everything, you organise an 'experience' for them, right? Well, save yourself the trouble of searching the internet for ideas – Melbourne is an oversized party bag full of wacky and wonderful things to do. Even if you're just looking for a new way to spend your weekend, you could be abseiling face first down the side of a building, mixing up a spell at a witch's house or tending to your personal veggie patch. Melbourne is definitely your oyster, people.

Hide & Seek Melbourne: Hit the Streets is for all locals and visitors who want to discover some different ways of 'experiencing' Melbourne. We've done our best to identify 40 of the most unique activities, both in the city centre and inner suburbs. The book is divided into five, colour-coded chapters: **LET'S GET PHYSICAL** (new ways to get the blood pumping, whether it be shaking your booty or beating an African drum); **CULTURE CLUB** (art, literature and film without the pretentiousness); **LET'S GO OUTSIDE** (how to be at one with nature); **MIXED BAG** (basically, any activities that didn't fit in the other four categories) and **RELAX MAX** (some original pampering and grooming options). There's something for everyone here, no matter what your tastes or interests. And, in all cases, we've tried to make sure that these experiences won't cost the earth.

I'd like to say thank you to the freelancers whose contributions have made this book possible: to Erika Budiman for her incredible design and excellent photographs, to Chris Groenhout and Rachel Lewis for their skilled photography, to Dale Campisi for his editorial expertise, and to our in-house cartographer Emily Maffei for her funky maps. Thanks also to the amazing team of in-the-know Melburnians who researched and wrote the reviews with such enthusiasm and dedication.

Finally, if you find somewhere else hidden or intriguing in Melbourne that you think others should seek out, please send us an email at **info@exploreaustralia.net.au**. Otherwise, there are a couple of blank pages at the back of the book for you to record your own discoveries as you hit the streets and explore this wonderful city.

Cheers,
Melissa Krafchek | Editor

ABOUT THE WRITERS

DALE CAMPISI

Dale publishes short reads and organises events about Australian history for Arcade Publications, which he does from his studio in the Nicholas Building. He is co-author of Explore Australia's *Go Explore Melbourne* deck of walking cards – the culmination of ten years exploring, eating and drinking on the streets of the 'Queen City of the South'.

DALE CAMPISI

MICHAEL BRADY

Michael is a Melbourne artist and 'gallerist'. He designs books and other material for Arcade Publications and is co-author of Explore Australia's *Go Explore Melbourne* deck of walking cards. He doesn't drive a car, so he walks a lot (which is a great way of getting to know the city). He enjoys observing the Bourke Street Mall from his balcony while dreaming of living in a gallery one day soon.

MICHAEL BRADY

JENNI KAUPPI

Melbourne's the kind of city you can fall in love with in a day. Well, that's how it was for Jenni when she moved here almost ten years ago. Luckily, her work as a food and travel writer has dovetailed nicely with her curiosity for this city's best hidey-holes.

JENNI KAUPPI

DAN TEO

Born in Singapore but bred in Melbourne, Dan loves all that his hometown has to offer, be it watching the footy on a cold winter's day, eating out at its many wonderful cafes and restaurants, or having a quiet Sunday tipple at a local pub. Dan is also a contributor to www.tummyrumbles.com.

DAN TEO

LUCY PERERA

Extreme curiosity, a penchant for bright, shiny objects and a nose for gastronomic goodness fuels Lucy's out-and-about bower bird ways. While travelling ten years ago, she happily discovered that people actually enjoyed her email epistles and has been writing ever since. Employed by the City of Melbourne, she enjoys the thrill of the chase for the next new thing.

VANESSA MURRAY

Vanessa is a freelance writer whose features, essays, reviews and other random outputs have been widely published in Australian newspapers and magazines. She has called Melbourne home for the past six years and loves its creative vibe, off-road bike paths and crazy weather. Her website is www.vanessa-murray.com.

RYAN SMITH

Ryan was born in Adelaide and made the obvious choice to move to Melbourne as soon as he possibly could. On any given day, you can find him playing with fabric swatches, trawling through thrift stores and flea markets for hidden treasures, reorganising his (or someone else's) apartment interior, or drinking Japanese beer at a corner table while feverishly filling notebooks with his scrawl.

MELLIE TEO

Mellie loves her hometown of Melbourne, which is just as well considering she lives, works and plays in the CBD. Being close to the action has its perks, especially when it fuels her interest in food writing and photography. Often found with laptop and digital camera at the ready, she captures her finds on www.tummyrumbles.com.

LUCY PERERA

VANESSA MURRAY

RYAN SMITH

MELLIE TEO

ABOUT THE WRITERS

SAMANTHA WILSON
Like so many Sandgropers before her, Sam traded in Perth's surf, sand and sun for Melbourne's culture, food and fun over six years ago and hasn't looked back. A freelance writer, she loves her adopted home primarily for its amazing people. But its buzzing music scene, endless film festivals, cool bars and fab vintage shops don't hurt either.

MATT DERODY
Matt has always lived in North Fitzroy, except for a year and a half in Japan and a year in Fitzroy. He loves the northern suburbs of Melbourne and when he's not feeling too modest, he'll go as far as calling himself NorthFitzroyalty. He speaks French, Japanese and English fluently and is currently studying a masters of editing and publishing.

LIOR OPAT
Humble foodie, erratic shopper, effusive cinephile and dependable coffee drinker, Lior is an unashamed culture junkie. And Melbourne keeps her well entertained with great music, coffee, food, theatre and access to films from all over the world. Every time she thinks she's seen it all, Melbourne makes her think again.

SARAH FRASER
Sarah grew up in country Victoria, where she ate roasts, rode tractors and drank instant coffee and VB. She has lived in Melbourne for more than ten years, and now eats char-grilled vegies, rides trams and drinks double-shot long macchiatos and micro-brewery beer. Melbourne has that effect on you.

SAMANTHA WILSON

MATT DERODY

LIOR OPAT

SARAH FRASER

OLIVER DRISCOLL

Oliver is a Melbourne-based short story writer and poet with an interest in teasing out the narratives enmeshed in the city's fabric. He can regularly be found weaving in and out of the streets and laneways – according to him this is a brilliant city to explore on foot.

KSENIA GOUREEVE

Ksenia travels constantly, and writes obsessively about the extraordinary and mundane phenomena of life. She has come to view everything as review fodder – from a coffee to a sunset. Her reviews take on a number of writing styles from professional and casual to rants with lots of CAPS lock.

MANDY WILDSMITH

Mandy has divided her life between tennis coaching and a world of books. Some say it's a bizarre mix, but after many cold winter nights coaching in legwarmers, she decided to become a sales rep peddling travel titles around Melbourne. Mandy's always been passionate about writing and most of her ideas are born with a latte in one hand and a pen in the other.

SAMUEL ZIFCHAK

Samuel grew up in Melbourne and, despite spending extensive periods of time overseas, finds he always heeds the call of his hometown. Having just returned from the UK, Sam will usually be found, soy latte cooling by his side, puzzling out rhymes in any of the wonderful cafes or bars that Melbourne is renowned for.

OLIVER DRISCOLL

KSENIA GOUREEVE

MANDY WILDSMITH

SAMUEL ZIFCHAK

LET'S GET PHYSICAL

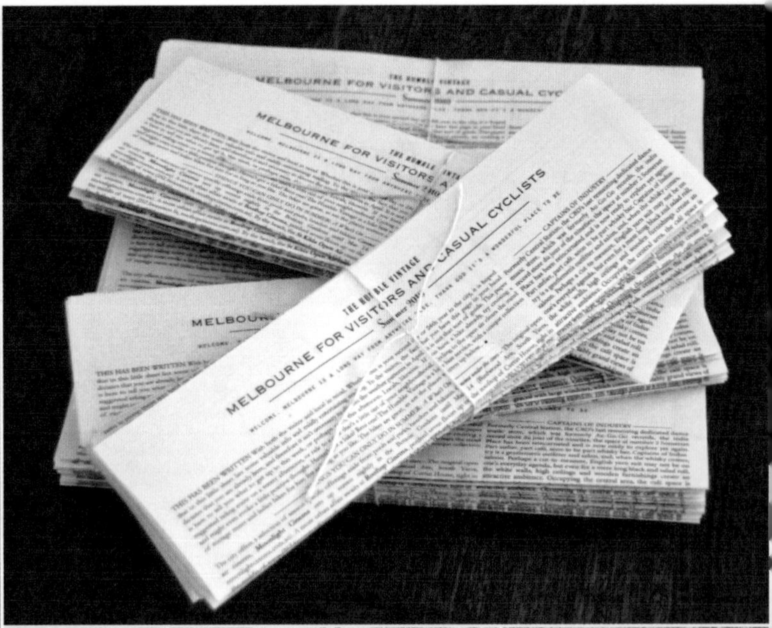
THE HUMBLE VINTAGE
MELBOURNE FOR VISITORS AND CASUAL CYCLISTS
CAPTAINS OF INDUSTRY

TICKET TO RIDE

Fixated on fixies* but can't afford one? Or just want a classier ride on which to peruse Melbourne's laneways on a Saturday? The Humble Vintage is here to help.

Helping tourists blend into Melbourne's bike scene since 2009, The Humble Vintage is a bike hire service that specialises in boutique bikes, with not a garishly coloured mountain bike in sight. Instead, you can hire the latest Dutch speed machine or a more sedate vintage ladies bike, complete with hand-woven (by the owner) wicker basket for that Bourke-Street-via-Cambridge vibe.

While there's no fixed shopfront for The Humble Vintage, there are pick-up points in the CBD, Fitzroy and St Kilda. With one phone call you can arrange a time and place for the handover and be freewheeling down the city's streets and lanes in no time. All bikes come with a helmet, lock, lights and a complimentary cycle guide to Melbourne, which conveniently includes bar and cafe reviews for stops along the recommended trails. So with map in hand you can check out some of Melbourne's sights or just stick to The Humble Vintage Cafe Trail, safe in the knowledge that you have the ultimate Sunday brunch accessory – a chic bike to park out the front.   **SARAH FRASER**

> **LET'S GET PHYSICAL**

0432 032 450
www.thehumblevintage.com

'ENCYCLO' TRIVIA
* Fixies are fixed-wheel bicycles that have no gears and often no brakes. They divide Melbourne's cycling community into those who think they're impractical and those who reckon they're the ultimate hipster accessory.

> LET'S GET PHYSICAL

NATIONAL INSTITUTE OF CIRCUS ARTS

BIG TRICKS FROM THE BIG TOP

Fed up with juggling the accounts? Your boss making you jump through hoops? Then run away and join the circus! NICA's short courses in tumbling, juggling, trapeze and other circus arts will fulfil those childhood dreams of the big top.

One of only a handful of circus training centres anywhere in the world, NICA's classes for regular folk are a novel way to keep fit, meet new people and exercise your creativity. The tumbling course is pretty much what it suggests – lessons in handstands and forward rolls, backward flips and somersaults, all to indulge your inner Chinese circus performer (not that you're likely to become *that* good). And for men who are ready to get in touch with their feminine side, the juggling course teaches the art of multi-tasking with clubs and knives.

Women especially like to get high on the flying trapeze, which is practised in a huge room that stands three storeys tall. The aerial preparation class takes in hoop, rope and cloudswing as well as trapeze. NICA welcomes folk of all ages and there's even a special class for the over 40s, meaning it's never too late to become a carny! LUCY PERERA

> LET'S GET PHYSICAL

41 Green St, Prahran
(03) 9214 6975
www.nica.com.au
Classes at various times throughout the week

See also
map 3 C2

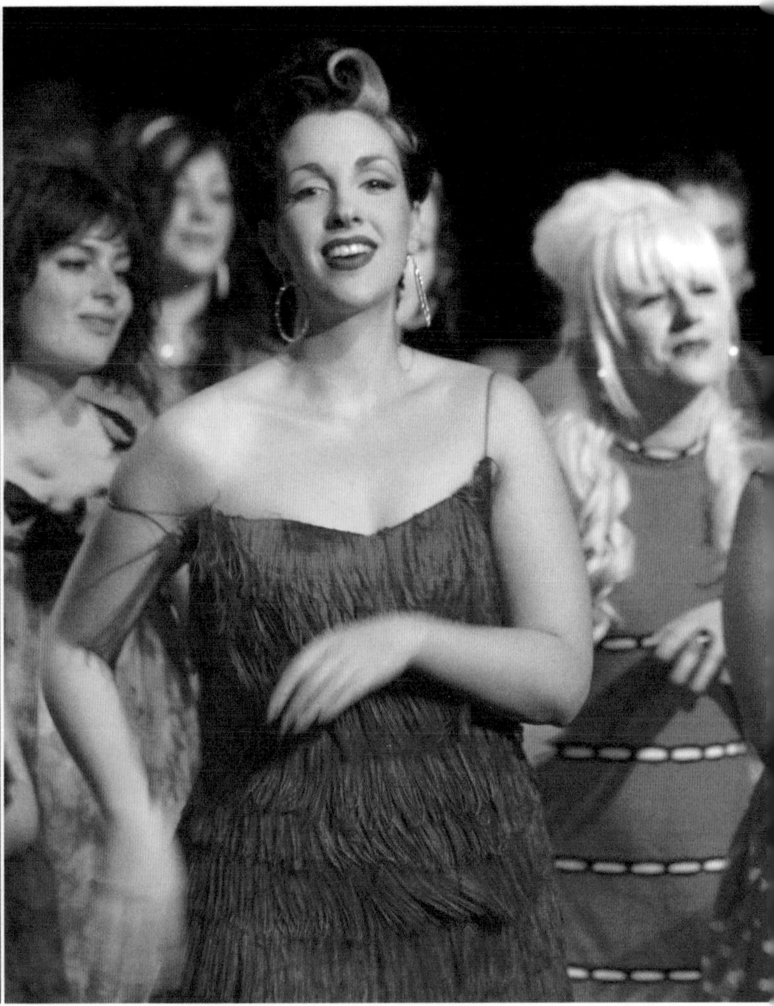

ALWAYS DANCEABLE, NEVER PREDICTABLE

Do the twist! Do the hully-gully! Do the Hillsong hands! Everything goes at Anna's Go-Go Academy, a weekly cardiac-boosting, butt-jiggling workout that's all about having a laugh and listening to some rockin' tunes while you watusi up a sweat.

In these unique classes, go-go guru Anna resurrects forgotten dance moves from the 1960s to a soundtrack that ranges from Elvis to the Detroit Cobras via Blondie, Normie Rowe and Ray Barretto. Two left feet? Relax. Nobody cares as long as you give it a red-hot crack – which is a major part of these classes' unpretentious charm. Young, old, female, male, straight, gay, hipster, square – they'll all be there alongside you, shaking it like the proverbial Polaroid picture.

But the main attraction is Anna herself. A modern-day Denise Drysdale*, the only thing bigger than Anna's hair is her personality. Dressed to kill in vintage mini-dresses and immaculate burlesque-bombshell make-up, she keeps up a running commentary throughout the classes, cracking endless jokes, singing along to the music and holding forth on subjects as diverse as perms, bingo wings*, her pet rabbit and Carmen Electra. As an added bonus, classes generally take place in a pub, so it probably won't be Gatorade you'll be drinking to keep up your fluids. **SAMANTHA WILSON**

> LET'S GET PHYSICAL

Various locations,
check the website for details
0402 769 515
www.gogoacademy.com.au

'ENCYCLO' TRIVIA

* Australian TV personality Denise 'Ding-Dong' Drysdale was Australia's premier go-go dancer in the 1960s.

* Bingo wings: floppy upper arms devoid of muscle tone, often seen on ladies who frequent bingo halls.

GO AHEAD AND JUMP!

They say that a fear of heights involves the fear that you might actually jump. Rap Jumping takes that fear, straps on a safety harness and leaps over the edge.

Australian Rappel Jumping is, put simply, abseiling face forwards. Also known as the karabiner rundown, it was invented in the 1960s by the Australian Army as a way to descend quickly – that is, face first. But don't think for a second that being safely tethered negates the adrenaline – it'll course through your body like a near-death experience.

Pioneer Macka Mackail has been running the world's only certified rappel jumping course for over 20 years. His relaxed, professional approach will put you at ease as you stare down a seven-storey building, allowing you to face that fear of what will happen after you step off the edge. The buzz comes with the second, third and fourth steps – and when you get to the bottom you want to go straight back up. Which is just as well because a session with Macka buys two jumps. So take up Van Halen's taunt: go ahead and jump! **MATT DERODY**

> **LET'S GET PHYSICAL**

334 City Rd, Southbank
1800 243 868
rapjumping.com.au
Jumps by appointment only

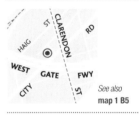

See also
map 1 B5

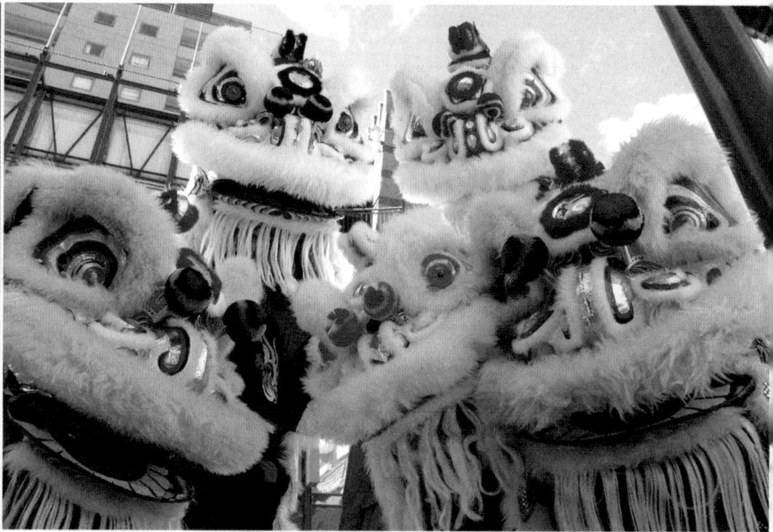

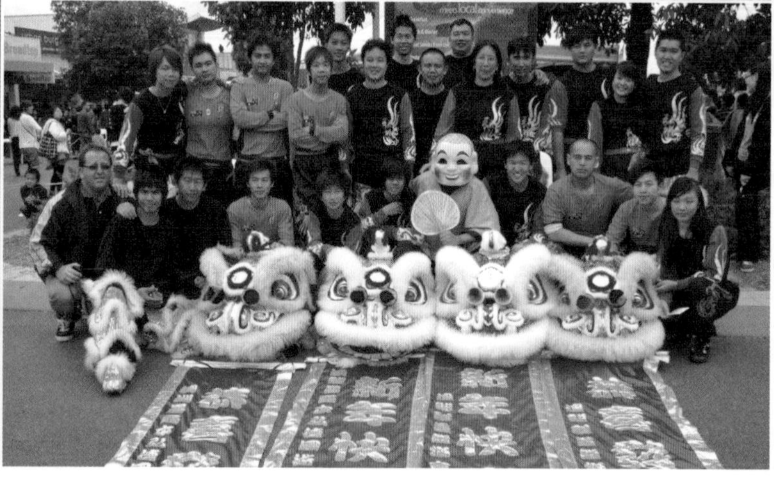

HONG DE LION DANCE ASSOCIATION

WARD OFF THOSE EVIL SPIRITS

The creation story of the lion dance is a rather fantastical one about a mythical beast that ravaged a village in China during the Han Dynasty. The locals rebelled – banging drums, setting off firecrackers, and scaring the heck out of the pesky beast with their very own acrobatically inclined dancing lion. Today, the lion dance is said to bring good luck and prosperity on auspicious occasions. And now you too can learn to dance like the big cat!

The lion dance is no heel and toe polka. It has more in common with martial arts and gymnastics; the movements mimic a lion's excitement, curiosity, caution, anger, happiness and playfulness. Made of paper-mâché and colourful cloth, the lion is controlled by two people – one in the head and one in the tail – who must learn to dance in unison to the rhythm of the drum, gong and cymbals. Together as one, the lion 'awakens' and seeks out food (commonly lettuce or oranges for good luck), which is strategically placed to make the lion climb, jump or move about cautiously to check for traps and ensure a safe path to the booty.

Melbourne's Hong De Lion Dance Association was formed in 2008 by a group of local enthusiasts. There is no charge for lessons (only for a uniform should you wish to continue), and guests are welcome to come along and have a go with no obligation to join. Instructors teach on a voluntary basis, so call ahead as classes are sometimes cancelled due to performances. **MELLIE TEO**

> ## LET'S GET PHYSICAL

Fusion Dance Studios,
Level 1, 478 Smith St, Fitzroy
0418 105 760
www.hongdelion.com.au
Open Sun 11am–3pm

See also
map 2 C5

> LET'S GET PHYSICAL

NORTH FITZROY BOWLING CLUB

THE SOCIABLE SPORT

For those who like to picnic, enjoy a bevvy and score points at the same time, lawn bowls is just the ticket. The Fitzroy Bowling Club offers lawn and ball hire in 2-hour blocks, and with two large greens (room for 18 groups) and six beer gardens (yes, Germany eat your heart out), your crowd can happily wile away the day mastering this centuries-old sport.

The basic premise of lawn bowls doesn't take too long to grasp: roll the ball as close to the jack (the little white ball) as you can. Just ask the staff – keen bowlers themselves – for handy handling tips to get the one-up on your mates.

Not interested in playing ends? Then just grab a drink from the bar, pull up a patch by the green and watch your mates battle it out in this most sociable of sports. Beer, wine and basic spirits are on offer throughout the day, as well as basic pub fare at night. The club is also open throughout winter, but to garner a true appreciation of what is on offer, the summer months are your best bet. Enjoy.   **SAMUEL ZIFCHAK**

> LET'S GET PHYSICAL

578 Brunswick St, North Fitzroy
(03) 9481 3137
www.fvbowls.com.au
Open Mon–Fri 12pm–late,
Sat 10am–late, Sun 11am–late

See also
map 2 C5

> LET'S GET PHYSICAL

PUTTING THE MOTOR IN JANE FONDA'S HONDA

Hands up who associates aerobics with day-glo lycra, leotards, legwarmers and tragic music? Jane Fonda has a lot to answer for! Luckily, the gang at Rock Aerobics are here to redress the balance, gleefully subverting those stale old clichés with a healthy dose of attitude and air guitar. If Joan Jett or Suzi Quatro* ever decided to hit the fitness circuit, this is where they'd rock out.

The inspiration for Rock Aerobics came to instructor Ambika in 2008 after she and some friends were bemoaning the dreadful soundtracks common to most aerobics classes. Hyper-produced dance pop may get the pulse racing, but Ambika reckons rock'n'roll is tailor-made for heart-thumping, fist-pumping aerobic action!

Whether you're pogo-ing to The Clash or punching the air to AC/DC, Rock Aerobics gives you the buzz of the mosh pit with the benefits of the gym. Sure, there's the traditional step-touches, knee-lifts and sit-ups thrown in, but it's the less conventional moves that make these classes so much fun. A bit of windmill guitar here, some high-energy skanking there and before you know it your muscle tone will be the envy of Iggy Pop.

Not surprisingly, the classes are much loved by the local rock-chick set. They also attract students, office workers and even mature folk, but as long as you bring a sense of humour and your best rock face you'll fit right in. But be prepared to work at it – just because these classes are held in a licensed venue doesn't mean you don't have to earn that beer first!

SAMANTHA WILSON

> ### LET'S GET PHYSICAL

Yah Yahs, 99 Smith St, Fitzroy
0405 576 310
rockaerobics.weebly.com
Open Thurs 7–8pm

See also map 1 G2

'ENCYCLO' TRIVIA
* Joan Jett and Suzi Quatro are both American female rock musicians, who wore leather in a very 'unfeminine' way for the 1970s.

CENTRE FOR WEST AFRICAN MUSIC AND CULTURE

FINDING THE BEAT OF YOUR OWN DRUM

St Kilda has always been home to the unexpected, so it should come as no surprise that it's here you'll find that little piece of Africa you've been looking for. At the Centre for West African Music and Culture – a one-stop shop for rhythm makers – you'll find the leathery aromas of hundreds of drums and the earthy and colourful tones of African textiles, arts, crafts and clothing.

Drumming classes and workshops are run with a visceral passion for the sound and rhythm of Africa, and are suitable for beginners, naturals and long-time drummers alike. Enthusiastic teachers from a range of musical backgrounds encourage even the most rhythmically challenged students to find their inner percussionist with their monthly dundun workshops. Here you'll learn core African drumming sequences and enjoy a bit of a jam too. The truly committed can try the six-week Djembe courses, retreats and even a drumming tour in Africa itself. Closer to home and fun for everyone, the weekly free-for-all jams are all about joining the tribe and finding your groove.

Once your left and right brain hemispheres have fully converged, there's also a range of dance classes from traditional African to Congolese Soukos, Afro Funk and capoeira. And you can dance to the beat of your own drum after a drum-making workshop. Whether you choose to drum, dance or just shop, the hypnotic rhythm of Africa is guaranteed to course through your veins for a long time to come. **JENNI KAUPPI**

> **LET'S GET PHYSICAL**

12 Grey St, St Kilda
(03) 9525 3073
www.africandrumming.com.au
Open Mon–Fri 10am–6pm,
Sat 10.30am–5pm

See also
map 3 B3

> LET'S GET PHYSICAL

DANCERS IN THE DARK

No lights, no lycra, no alcohol, no teacher and not a great deal of socialising either. It may cost you $5 to join in, but it's far from contrived and quite a bit clandestine. So what is it?

No Lights No Lycra is a weekly dance jam that started right here in Melbourne and has since inspired similar outfits in Brooklyn and Berlin. All that's asked of you is that you unleash your inner interpretive dancer, un-tether your trip-hopper and let your spirit fingers sparkle among an amorphous blur of silhouettes with arms and legs akimbo. Fuelled by endorphins and lit only by the glow of a laptop, this is a decidedly anti-nightclub dance experience: the two venues in Fitzroy and Brunswick East are relatively bare community centres, and there's never a strobe light in sight.

The music is joyously random (from Edith Piaf to commercial R'n'B and *Hakuna Matata**), meaning you're bound to love and hate something at least once in your 90-minute session. But in spite of a few poor music choices, the experience will leave you feeling completely liberated – like you've poured out your heart to a non-judgmental stranger. So whether you know *how* to dance or you breakdance like a crab, get down to it in the dark.

JENNI KAUPPI

> LET'S GET PHYSICAL

250 George St, Fitzroy
Open Tues 7–8.30pm

49 Nicholson St, Brunswick East
Open Wed 7–8.30pm
nolightsnolycra.blogspot.com

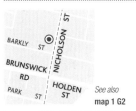

See also
map 1 G2

See also
map 2 C3

'ENCYCLO' TRIVIA
* *Hakuna Matata* is a song from the popular Disney movie *The Lion King*.

CULTURE CLUB

> CULTURE CLUB

FOR LITERARY ALLSORTS

Reading is to Melbourne what peanuts are to butter and jelly. And though it might be a little bit ironic that we'd build a shrine to what is predominantly a solitary pursuit, The Wheeler Centre has become a magnet for the city's literati.

Nestled in the side of the State Library of Victoria on Little Lonsdale Street, The Wheeler Centre is home to local literary organisations and a very busy events space. There's something on almost every night of the week – from author talks to public debates, book launches and poetry readings. Best of all, most events are free.

The program is diverse: from literary luminaries like Peter Carey to pop culturists such as Bret Easton Ellis. But it isn't all art-fart-poop-tit. Melbourne's emerging writers feature prominently, and the program is peppered with alternatives such as the Writer's Mix Tape, which looks at the popular music that influences writers; a weekly lunchtime soapbox, which Melburnians have enjoyed in one form or another since the 1850s; and even literary speed dating for those looking to curl up with more than a good book.

LUCY PERERA

> ## CULTURE CLUB

176 Lt Lonsdale St, Melbourne
(03) 9094 7800
www.wheelercentre.com
Opening hours dependent on events

See also
map 1 D3

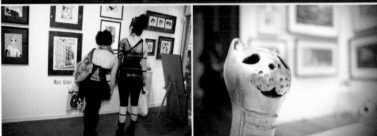

OUTRÉ GALLERY

ART THAT GOES POP!

Never boring, always original and entirely out of the ordinary, Outré Gallery is where lovers of lowbrow and counter-culture go to flirt with art appreciation. Playing host to regular exhibitions of contemporary art from around the world, Outré Gallery also stocks street art magazines, pop paraphernalia and designer toys – a fusion that means it doesn't intimidate like a commercial art gallery.

For under $100 you can pick up a poster, painting, book or curio to suit even the most esoteric of tastes. The art on display here ranges from retro pop, street art and graffiti to surrealism, folk and tiki (to name just a very few). Gallery faves include Dutch artist Angelique Houtkamp, who creates nostalgic sweetheart tattoo designs, and the much-adored Josh 'Shag' Agle, whose illustrative style channels the martini-quaffing headiness of the '50s and '60s.

And if you're looking for something distinctly Melbourne you can't go past the folksy works of Beci Orpin, the imaginative and surreal watercolours of Martin Harris, the mid-century animal ceramics of Gus McLaren or the gallery's resident pop art painter Gemma Jones. Make haste: a new love affair awaits! MELLIE TEO

> **CULTURE CLUB**

249 Elizabeth St, Melbourne
(03) 9642 5455
www.outregallery.com
Open Mon–Thurs 10.30am–5.30pm,
Fri 10.30am–7pm, Sat 10.30am–5pm,
Sun 12–4pm

See also
map 1 D4

> CULTURE CLUB

THE ART OF THE SIGN

You might rarely notice it, but typography runs your life. Every day it tells you where to go and gives you the lowdown on the important stuff, but rarely do we think of it as art.

Stephen Banham, a gentleman typographer who in the 1990s waged war against that pandemic typeface Helvetica, sees beauty in the typographic form. He also uses type as a way to see the city, peeling back the layers to reveal its graphic design.

Characters & Spaces, a free walking tour available online and in print, explores the social and cultural aspects of graphic design and typography. What it reveals are some great stories you've probably never stopped to notice. Like the quintessentially Aussie but thoroughly modernist mural above a strip club on Elizabeth Street, commissioned to project the image of a progressive city; or the anti-consumerist message in a feature wall of a busy shopping arcade; or the advertising site on the Victorian Heritage Register. There are also 'Adventure' questions throughout the guide, which make this a fun activity if you want to play a little hide and seek in the city. **DALE CAMPISI**

> **CULTURE CLUB**

www.characterevent.com

> CULTURE CLUB

FEMALE TALENT SCOUTING

Nothing says Melbourne like the crumbling grandeur of a Victorian building. Disused and gone to seed until a recent refurbishment, the Crossley Building at the top of Bourke Street has been a butcher shop, slaughter yard and home to the colonial landscape artist Eugene von Guérard. Today it rubs shoulders with local legends like Italian eatery Pellegrini's, The Paperback Bookshop, fabric stalwarts Job Warehouse, Von Haus bar and jewellery store Glitzern.

All that was missing from this building's history was an art gallery. Enter Sarah Scout in all her old-world charm: creaking floorboards, elaborate tiled fireplace and tree-top views over Bourke Street. Like a lost earring found, Sarah Scout is a pleasing discovery, an intimate gallery with a distinctly feminist grounding. There's a focus on representing emerging and established female artists, as well as showcasing conceptual art*. The Thursday night exhibition openings attract Melbourne's bright young art types to experience the range of thought-provoking pieces on display.

But don't go inquiring after Sarah herself. She's a composite personality named for the children of curators Vikki McInnes and Kate Barber – a phantom personality that hints at the curators' constant search for new talent and one that underpins the feminine feel of the gallery and the work on show.

JENNI KAUPPI

> CULTURE CLUB

Level 1, 1A Crossley St, Melbourne
(03) 9654 4429
www.sarahscoutpresents.com
Open Thurs–Fri 11am–6pm, Sat 12–5pm

See also
map 1 E3

'ENCYCLO' TRIVIA
* Conceptual art stems from the notion that art is about ideas, not so much the physical forms that contain them. It moves away from traditional mediums and can be realised in many forms such as 3D installations.

YOU WON'T BE SHORT-CHANGED

What should you do when you take over a massive warehouse that used to be a Harley Davidson assembly factory? Why, convert it into a cafe, set up a gallery, install a cinema and make it all available for the city's creative types to hold exhibitions, film festivals and magazine launches, of course! The chameleonic 1000 £ Bend does just that.

On weekdays the cafe serves excellent organic fair-trade coffee and inexpensive food (around $10) for breakfast and lunch. With free wi-fi and access to power points, you can study or work in shabby-chic style on the comfy retro couches or in the outdoor cell overlooking Little Lonsdale Street. By night the massive rear space – replete with caravan, but a long way from cramped – plays host to exhibitions, launches and even second-hand garage sales.

Upstairs is a 160-seat cinema playing all manner of short and long films. There's always something interesting going on here, so it pays to check the website regularly for event details, times and prices. One thing is for sure, if you're looking to tap into Melbourne's independent and underground scene, this is a good place to start.   **DAN TEO**

> ## CULTURE CLUB

361 Lt Lonsdale St, Melbourne
www.thousandpoundbend.com.au
Open Mon–Fri 8am–7pm,
Sat–Sun 11am–7pm

See also
map 1 D3

> CULTURE CLUB

A STITCHIN' TIME

Knitting is gnarly, crochet is cool, and come Sunday afternoon in Melbourne you can't turn around in a cafe without being poked in the eye with a 6 millimetre steel-core yarn integration implement. This isn't some nanna apocalypse; it's grandma chic and it's sweeping Melbourne like a cable-knit sweater.

For those keen but uninitiated into the world of plain, purl, yo, ch1 and hdc2tog, Coffee, Cake, Crochet, Knitting (CCCK) is a great place to start. It's a boutique yarn store that offers much more than balls of wool. You can browse their impressive range of yarns – from bamboo to organic merino to milk-protein blends – or, if you dare, engage the shop assistant in a discussion on the psychology of knitting or the evils of acrylics. Or, more prosaically, get some advice on your crochet technique.

CCCK runs knitting classes for groups and individuals, and staff guarantee you'll learn to knit, whether it takes 1 hour or 4 hours. Once you're feeling up to it, you might want to curl up with a funky pattern book on the comfy 'knitters' lounge and try out your newly purchased possum/alpaca blend. On the other hand, the lounge is a perfect place to have a cuppa and spin an entirely different type of yarn. Invite some friends for a stitch 'n' bitch – just leave the cheap acrylic at home. **SARAH FRASER**

> **CULTURE CLUB**

234 High St, Northcote
(03) 9481 6339
www.ccck.com.au
Open Mon–Sun 10am–6pm

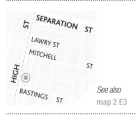

See also
map 2 E3

WE MAKE STUFF GOOD
STREET ART & BAR TOURS

GOOD TO GO

Ordinarily we wouldn't recommend you go down dark alleys with strangers, but we encourage you to make an exception to your stranger-danger rule for the guys and gals of We Make Stuff Good (WMSG). A collective of artists and designers, these guys will be your best mates for a few hours as they show you around the city's bar and street-art scenes.

Famous though Melbourne may be for its street art, the city actually has some pretty tough anti-graffiti laws – even the handiwork of prolific British artist Banksy* and French artist Space Invader is not appreciated by the law. Which is what got WMSG thinking about running tours of the scene to show that it's art, not crime. At 4.5 hours these tours are long, but they meander over the entire CBD and Fitzroy, and finish with dinner at a dumpling house in Chinatown. Groups are small, giving the experience an intimacy you won't get jostling around with a busload of tourists, following a megaphone-carrying guide. Indeed, your guide will be a Melbourne artist, so you're guaranteed to come away with some real insights into this semi-permanent world of art. Great value at just $40 a pop.

The bar tour takes you through some of Melbourne's hard-to-find venues, with a free drink at every stop. You can make a day of it by combining the two tours into one whopping day of city cruising – and they'll even cut you a mate's rate. **JENNI KAUPPI**

> **CULTURE CLUB**

0413 943 528
www.wemakestuffgood.com
Street art tours Sat 3–7.30pm;
Bar tours Wed, Fri & Sat 7.30pm–12am

'ENCYCLO' TRIVIA
* Working under the radar, Banksy is the pseudonym of the world's most famous graffiti artist. His often satirical and political works have graced city walls around the world (including Melbourne).

> CULTURE CLUB

THE NICHOLAS BUILDING

NINE FLOORS OF CREATIVITY

Every artist knows someone who's had a studio in the Nicholas Building. It's like a rite of passage for Melbourne's creative community. The building may be a little bit decrepit, but the rent is cheap and it's charmingly idiosyncratic – having been a mixed-use building since it was built for Aspro king Alfred Nicholas in the 1920s.

The array of occupants is dizzying, as the directory in Cathedral Arcade (look up for the stained glass ceiling) will attest. Most studios are private, so be prepared to encounter a lot of closed doors. Thursdays through Saturdays are the best days to visit; and a highlight of a weekday trip is a vertical ride with the city's last remaining lift attendants Joan and Dimi, whose workplaces are like microcosms of their lives. They'll take you to Stephen McLaughlan's experimental art gallery on level 8, and you'll find artist-run initiative Blindside on level 7.

Level 2 will keep you entertained for hours with vintage haberdashery L'Ucello, button mecca Buttonmania, recycled craft boutique Harold and Maude, and Japanese textile specialists Kimono House. Pigment Gallery shows the works of emerging artists, and on level 1 you'll find the stalwart poetry and ideas bookshop, Collected Works.

Once a year all nine floors participate in Open Studios – a two-day stickybeak event where you can wander through the entire building, meet the myriad artists, designers, jewellers, milliners and publishers, and buy direct from the makers. **MICHAEL BRADY**

> CULTURE CLUB

37 Swanston St, Melbourne
thenicholasbuilding.blogspot.com

See also
map 1 E4

> CULTURE CLUB

NO NO GALLERY

FINDING WAYS TO SAY 'YES'

It begins with a young art enthusiast finding a space. Art enthusiast makes commissions and accepts proposals for works he loves, by artists he admires. He lets people know about it, so they can come and have a look. People come, enjoy what they see, and they let other people know. Before young art enthusiast knows it, the space is a gallery.

You'll find No No by its distinct pink entrance down a side street in the inner-city suburb of North Melbourne, known for its Victorian architecture, working-class roots and mixed-bag demographic of the high and mighty, down and outers, students and immigrants. And it's this collision of cultures that makes it an interesting place to engage in the experimental arts.

Not for profit and curator run, the gallery is director Roger Nelson's way of saying 'yes' to nurturing emerging artists of the experimental kind. From one exhibition to the next, the work on show here is eclectic, diverse and often hard to define. This deliberate category evasion is probably the gallery's most uniting theme, so expect the unexpected from photo collages to tapestry and art made from expandable foam and balsa wood.

Suddenly, the young art enthusiast is spoiled for choice with everything from craft-based exhibitions to ad-hoc film screenings, and No No Gallery continues to be an ideal space for it all. **JENNI KAUPPI**

> **CULTURE CLUB**

14 Raglan St, North Melbourne
0405 968 618
www.nonogallery.org
Open Thurs–Sat 12–6pm

See also
map 1 B2

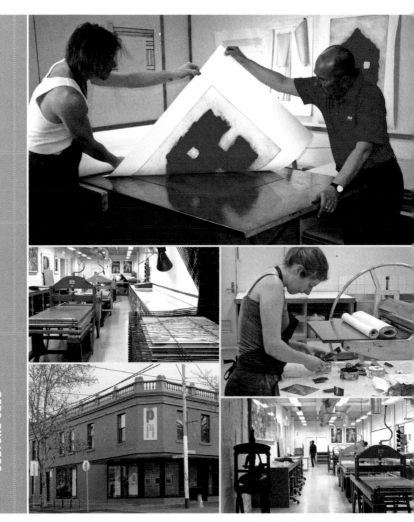

THE PRINCE OF PRINTS

In a wireless world of laptops, smartphones and e-reading devices, printing seems a little bit redundant. But dead? Pfft! The Australian Print Workshop shows that printing is an art that will never die. Starting out in a rundown shopfront, the workshop has weathered three decades of change on Fitzroy's Gertrude Street. Now surrounded by galleries, boutiques and fancy eateries, a recent facelift has made the printmaking room visible from the street – revealing some pretty impressive vintage equipment that will get you wondering about how it all works.

Inside, the open studio provides even the most humble artist or novice with access to all the tools you need for etching, lithography, relief printing and monoprinting. Workshops and classes with experienced printmakers run year-round, so you too can learn everything from printing techniques to making bona fide books of your own.

But if getting dirty ain't your thing, there's a crisp clean gallery of contemporary printmaking for you to ogle with your hands behind your back. Group guided tours will help you develop your appreciation for this most industrial of arts, and take in the current show and printing demonstrations. There's also a huge selection of stored prints available to buy as well as a bargain box full of cut-price treasures.

For those who say print is dead, take a look.

MICHAEL BRADY

> CULTURE CLUB

210 Gertrude St, Fitzroy
(03) 9419 5466
www.australianprintworkshop.com
Open Tues–Fri 10am–5pm, Sat 12–5pm

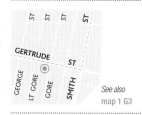

See also
map 1 G3

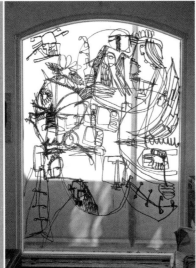

UNTIL-NEVER GALLERY

THE ART GALLERY FOR PEOPLE WHO HATE ART GALLERIES

A visit to Until Never kind of feels like going to an underground gig your parents wouldn't approve of. But climbing the dingy stairs past the graffiti, tags, stickers and stencils of Rutledge and Hosier lanes instead takes you to an independent gallery full of underground art (ironically located on the second floor).

Until Never evolved organically from a mishmash studio for artists whose works spilled out onto the street and then back into the building in gallery form. While exhibitions vary from street art to fine art, photography, sculpture, performance and installation, the one thing they have in common is what gallery director Andy Mac describes as the punk attitude of do-it-yourself raw invention. The ever-changing interior has seen works by local, interstate and international artists ranging in age from 16 to 60 years old.

But don't just look inside, Hosier Lane is like another part of the gallery, with artists often creating a piece for the alley too. Here you'll find models on a shoot, hipsters with serious zoom lenses and tourists mouth-open, ogling the now world-famous walls. You'll find comic art, stencils, political statements and tiny details that will make you think or laugh out loud.

But before you step into Until Never Gallery, take a deep breath and leave your preconceptions about art and culture at the door. Exhibitions at Until Never are not there to conform to your world view – they're there to challenge and enhance it.   **KSENIA GOUREEVE**

> **CULTURE CLUB**

Level 2, 3–5 Hosier La, Melbourne
(03) 9663 0442
www.untilnever.net
Open Wed–Sat 12–6pm

See also
map 1 E4

> CULTURE CLUB

LYON HOUSEMUSEUM

HOUSE FIRST, MUSEUM SECOND?

While most of us think of home as a private place, the Lyon family have opened theirs up to the public. But then they don't live in an ordinary house. Located on a nondescript street in the Melbourne suburb of Kew, architect Corbett Lyon has created the Lyon Housemuseum – a place to display just some of the contemporary Australian art he and his wife Yueji have collected over the past two decades.

There are works by many of Australia's leading contemporary artists including Patricia Piccinini, Scott Redford and Callum Morton, and Howard Arkley's 17-panel *Fabricated Rooms* takes prime position in the upstairs dining room. But perhaps the oddest feature of the museum is the family itself. Their living areas flow around the museum spaces, and the museum sometimes flows into their living space – challenging conventional perceptions of what's public and what's private.

Built around the White Box (literally a white space given over to art) and its evil twin the Black Box (a dark space for media art screenings as well as cartoons and movies for their kids' sleepovers), the house is a sprawling testament to modern architecture. Some timber walls and ceilings are covered with text that makes up a story the family wrote (incidentally, the text is arranged to spell out ART) and doors are strategically placed to hide bedrooms when the family does want a bit of privacy. Tours book out months in advance, so plan ahead to peek inside the Lyons' house. RYAN SMITH

> CULTURE CLUB

219 Cotham Rd, Kew
(03) 9817 2300
www.lyonhousemuseum.com.au
Check website for openings
(bookings essential)

See also map 1 J2

AUSTRALIAN CENTRE FOR THE MOVING IMAGE

FILM FANS HEAD TO FED SQ

These days 'museum' and 'exhibition' mean a whole lot more than quiet rooms, old scholars and obvious tourists with their hands behind their backs, quietly discussing brush strokes. The Australian Centre for the Moving Image is a world of screen-based art that is like heaven for film junkies and gamers.

It's funny to think that the world's most culturally pervasive – and certainly its most profitable – art form only recently got its first dedicated museum space. Fortunately for Melburnians, the phenomenon of the film museum landed in Melbourne with the opening of ACMI (for the acronym-inclined) in 2002. The permanent exhibition *Screen Worlds: The Story of Film, Television and Digital Culture* is a free interactive overview of the development of the moving image – from film to video game and all the mash-ups in between. Young and old will flip out at the classic and contemporary video games, which you can play for free! There are also free tours departing daily at 11am and 2pm. The subterranean galleries host regular themed exhibitions about technology and media, as well as some incredibly successful touring exhibitions including *Pixar: 20 Years of Animation* and *Tim Burton*, fresh from its stint at MoMA in New York.

ACMI also boasts two high-tech cinemas, playing documentaries, cult films and classics that you won't see at the multiplex. And just as amazing is the Australian Mediatheque – a digital archive of Australian television and film that TV and movie buffs can access any day of the week.

RYAN SMITH

> CULTURE CLUB

Federation Sq, Melbourne
(03) 8663 2200
www.acmi.net.au
Open Mon–Sun 10am–6pm

See also
map 1 E4

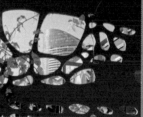

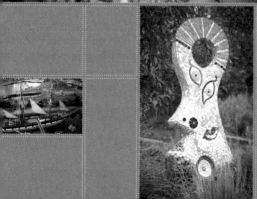

LET'S GO OUTSIDE

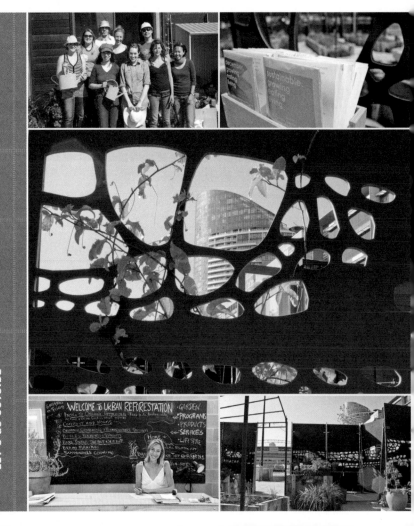

URBAN REFORESTATION

SUSTAINABILITY WITH STYLE

Sustainability is the buzzword of the noughties, but it doesn't have to mean mud-brick houses and prayer flags. Urban Reforestation, located in Melbourne's hyper-modern Docklands precinct, is a global design project that aims to inspire local apartment dwellers to live sustainably in a very approachable way.

Juxtaposed against the concrete and glass towers that surround it, this new community hub connects locals over sprouting herbs and veggies. It's also a top spot to sit and enjoy a chai latte and soak up some community spirit in the sunshine. There's an eco-shop that sells plants, seeds and gardening tools, as well as an education centre for classes on organic and balcony gardening, composting, worm farms, bread-making, beer brewing and home cooking. Even if you're not a Docklander, you'll find something useful to create your own little green oasis at home.

The friendly staff at Urban Reforestation are always happy to chat about the project's benefits and vision, so drop by or check their website for the latest info on what's happening in Melbourne's waterside neighbourhood, where the future's looking most definitely green.

DAN TEO

> LET'S GO OUTSIDE

Cnr Geographe Street & Keera Way, Docklands
www.urbanreforestation.com
Garden open 24 hrs; Shop open Mon & Thurs–Fri 10am–5pm, Tues 2–5.30pm

See also map 1 A5

> LET'S GO OUTSIDE

VEG OUT COMMUNITY GARDENS

NOT YOUR GARDEN VARIETY GARDEN

The tranquil setting of Veg Out Community Gardens is the green jewel in the racing heart of bayside St Kilda. While visitors eat, drink, sunbathe and party hard nearby, green-thumbed locals are busily tending their garden plots.

This herb and veggie oasis draws quite a crowd on Sundays, when the gardens are full of families, rabbits and chickens, and there's often a barbie on the go (the gardeners come as much to catch up with friends and neighbours over a cuppa on a deck chair as to tend to their plots).

It's easy to get caught up in the spirit of helping out here, so if you feel inspired, see one of the guys in charge and ask for a job: there's always a scarecrow to stuff or an escaped quail to find, and as a worker you might even score a delicious lunch from the garden kitchen.

If community bonding isn't your thing visit the gardens on a weekday when you can mosey about the garden plots in relative solitude. These gardens are brimming with personality – and guaranteed to inspire you to cultivate your own little patch of earth.   KSENIA GOUREEVE

> LET'S GO OUTSIDE

Cnr Shakespeare Gr & Chaucer St,
St Kilda
www.vegout.asn.au
Open Mon–Sun sunrise–sunset

See also
map 3 B4

> LET'S GO OUTSIDE

AUSTRALIAN NATIVE GARDEN, ROYAL PARK

AUSSIE JEWEL IN THE ROYAL PARK CROWN

Royal Park is a whole lot of park – almost 200 hectares in fact – and it's just 3 kilometres from the CBD. It's got a memorial cairn to explorers Burke and Wills*, zoological gardens, a golf course, cricket pitches, wetlands, numerous walking tracks and a little Aussie oasis that makes for the perfect spot to escape the city and soak up some genuine Australiana without risking your neck or your fashion sense.

Designed by renowned Australian landscape architect Grace Fraser in 1977, the Australian Native Garden is at the south-eastern entrance to Royal Park. You can wander among river red gum trees, shrubs and flora indigenous to Melbourne, such as native daisies, kangaroo paw and those bell-shaped flowers, correas. The pond is an excellent place for birdwatchers, picnickers, day-trippers, hula hoopers and lizard spotters alike.

The designers of greater Royal Park envisioned 'a place where the Earth swells, the dome of the sky soars overhead, and the horizon beckons'. Today we've got sweeping views, prolific wildlife and age-old eucalypts in a bush setting just 10 minutes from town. If Skippy* was a city dweller, this is where she'd come to remind herself of home.

JENNI KAUPPI

> ### LET'S GO OUTSIDE

Gatehouse St, Parkville
(03) 9388 9722

See also
map 2 A5

'ENCYCLO' TRIVIA

* Burke and Wills were 19th-century explorers who famously died trying to find a route from Melbourne through to the very north of Australia. The cairn in Royal Park commemorates the starting point of their expedition in 1860.

* Skippy is the kangaroo star of the iconic Australian 1960s TV show, *Skippy, The Bush Kangaroo*.

> LET'S GO OUTSIDE

TRANSFORMING THE YARRA

AGAINST THE FLOW

The history of Melbourne's Yarra River has been a turbulent one: its course was straightened and its rapids blasted away in the 19th century, which left it salty and dirty, and led to a century of neglect as a sewer for the city's industry. Even today Melburnians approach the Yarra's brown, murky water with a fear of disease – when tennis star Jim Courier went for a dip in the river to celebrate winning the Australian Open in 1992, most probably thought he'd emerge with a second head.

But since the 1980s, planners, architects and activists have pushed for change, so that the city may come to embrace its river. Transforming the Yarra is a series of five podcast walking tours that give insight into the changes the Yarra has seen and felt, the people involved, how it's increasingly becoming a site for recreational areas, and the unrealised visions for the waterfront – like the artists' colony that could have been built instead of Crown Casino (thanks Jeff Kennett*).

The tour departs from Federation Square and takes in Princes Bridge, Southbank Promenade, Queens Bridge and Duke and Orr's Dry Dock at the Convention and Exhibition Centre. Early evening is the best time to go, when the public art is illuminated, the wide walkways are scattered with busking musicians and performers, and the promenade and low arched footbridges are bathed in the city's lights.

OLIVER DRISCOLL

> **LET'S GO OUTSIDE**

**www.majorprojects.vic.gov.au/
transforming-the-yarra**

'ENCYCLO' TRIVIA
* Jeff Kennett was premier of Victoria between 1992 and 1999. His interest in opening the biggest casino in the Southern Hemisphere was very controversial.

> LET'S GO OUTSIDE

CERES

IT'S SO EASY BEING GREEN

Like the Roman grain goddess that shares its name, CERES* (pronounced 'series') has a practical Earth mother vibe to it. And this isn't just because this patch of green is a well-established community environment park – it's also reflected in its 'open during daylight hours' policy, eschewing modern timekeeping altogether.

Native nursery, cafe, bar, market, community veggie garden, green technology centre, bike workshop – CERES has something for everyone from compulsive composters, recyclers and growers to cyclists and solar energy enthusiasts. On Saturday mornings, locals converge on the market to fill their string shopping bags with delicious organic veggies, recycled clothing, second-hand books, live music and a beaut view over the free-range chicken run down to Merri Creek. The park also offers dozens of workshops and courses from beekeeping to home brewing.

If all that sounds exhausting, you can just slip into the cafe and do your bit with an organic latte and one of the best muffins in Brunswick. There's also the new Merri Table & Bar that serves tapas-style meals made from local seasonal produce.

The beauty of CERES is that it's more than just the sum of its parts. It attracts everyone from old hippies to inner-city hipsters and suburban families alike, and you're guaranteed to leave with a warm, fuzzy, 100% renewable glow.

SARAH FRASER

> **LET'S GO OUTSIDE**

Cnr Roberts & Stewart sts,
Brunswick East
(03) 9389 0100
www.ceres.org.au
Open during daylight hours;
Cafe open Mon–Fri 8.30am–4pm,
Sat 8.30am–5pm, Sun 9am–5pm;
Organic market open Wed 9am–1pm,
Fri 9am–5pm (shop only), Sat 9am–1pm

*See also
map 2 C2*

'ENCYCLO' TRIVIA
* Roman goddess aside, CERES also stands for Centre for Education and Research in Environmental Strategies.

MIXED BAG

SECRET SCREENINGS

Forget the comforts of the multiplex; the best way to see cinema these days is so far out of your comfort zone you won't even know where you're going until hours before the lights go down! This is cinema like you've never experienced, complete with film-specific dress code and accompanying performance artists.

Underground Cinema works on the ideas of spontaneity and maximum immersion. The experience begins after you sign up to the website and await the email about the next screening. You won't be told what the movie is, you'll only be given clues about the genre and how to dress – maybe Victorian peasant, '80s horror or New York beat.

Supplemented by performances, music and elaborate sets, screenings take place in a different venue each month and are adapted to suit each film. When they screened parkour* documentary *Generation Yamakasi*, the Underground Cinema team erected scaffolding for performers to scale and leap between. They commandeered a church to screen Tim Burton's *Sleepy Hollow*, transforming the garden into a graveyard. They've had hip-hop dancers and skate boarders, and spray-painted cars and warehouses.

Film fans go all out dressing up for these events – making it at times unclear who is staff and who is patron. All this puts the film in a new light, making a trip to the flicks a wild and unpredictable event.

OLIVER DRISCOLL

> **MIXED BAG**

www.undergroundcinema.com.au

'ENCYCLO' TRIVIA
* Parkour is the practice of negotiating the obstacles of the urban environment by climbing, jumping, dodging and so forth.

> MIXED BAG

PUGS IN THE PARK

Bred to adorn the lap of an ancient Chinese sovereign, pugs are at their cutest en masse in a public park. A posse of pugs frolicking joyously is pure, heart-melting cuteness: those chocolate-drop eyes, sweet squashy faces and curly-wurly tails just make you all gooey on the inside.

Perri the Pug, the monarch of Pugwood (the weekly gathering of Melbourne's pug populace), is a soulful-looking nine-year-old who's survived cancer, starred in a Doritos advertisement and is something of a celebrity on the local pooch scene. One of just four pugs at Pugwood's inaugural meeting almost a decade ago, Perri is still a regular at picturesque Elsternwick Park, although these days she's content to sit serenely and hold court, leaving the livelier shenanigans to younger pals like Ruby, Roly, China and Monty. And boy, are they lively! Get ready to coo when you see 30 or more of these little sweeties jumping, snuffling and running amok.

Pugwood's numbers swell during warmer months (their special Christmas get-together attracts hundreds of the little duffers) when, not surprisingly, the cute factor cranks into overdrive. Even if you're not a pug owner you're most welcome to watch – just rustle up a few friends, pack a picnic brunch and a camera, and get ready to squeal.

SAMANTHA WILSON

> **MIXED BAG**

Elsternwick Park, (enter via Head St), Elwood
www.freewebtown.com/pugwood
Open Sun from 10am

See also
map 3 D5

> MIXED BAG

NEILL MARTIN SHOE SHINE

SPIT-SHINE PERFECTION WHILE YOU WAIT

You can tell a lot about a person by the shoes they wear – and those shoes can say a lot when you can see your reflection in them. Located outside Harrolds department store at the Paris End of Collins Street (there are also two other locations in the CBD), Neill Martin Shoe Shine cleans and polishes your favourite treads (handbags too), ensuring you're looking your best for business meetings or a night on the town.

All you need to do is grab a seat at one of the two traditional shoe shine chairs and Neill will take care of the rest. You can read the paper while he gets to work, or if you're super busy just drop your shoes off for same-day pick-up. The basic clean and polish costs just $7. A premium polish is also available and for a little extra Neill will even take care of your suede shoes if you haven't been.

Neill himself is an inspirational character. Having confronted alcoholism and homelessness, Harrolds and the Salvation Army helped him regain control of his life when he hit upon the idea to combine the old-world craft of shoe shining with Melbourne's penchant for small businesses with a social conscience. Regulars at his stand are glad he did. Not only do they get their scuffed shoes polished, but honest Neill also regales them with a tale to remember. Indulge yourself here and your shoes will thank you.

DAN TEO

> **MIXED BAG**

101 Collins St, Melbourne
0438 305 030
Open Mon–Fri 10am–5pm

See also
map 1 E4

> MIXED BAG

KISS PIZZA

KISS 'N' TELL

It's a tough world out there for a local radio station. Not only does it have to compete with TV, cinema, CDs, DVDs, MP3s and anything that piques the imagination of those clever people at Apple, it also has to compete with those commercial radio stations that get all the attention.

Melbourne's dedicated dance music station, Kiss FM, must have known that the next sense after sound has to be taste, and so in the shadow of a railway line sits the Kiss FM motherhub with its own pizza restaurant, serving up thin-crust pizzas while you listen to their party tracks.

The delicious pizzas are fairly cheap (on Thursday nights, small pizzas are $5 if you name a Kiss FM frequency when you order). Expect to see usual suspects like margherita and capricciosa sharing the menu with slightly classier crusts like haloumi cheese, truffle oil and white pepper. Superstar DJ Carl Cox even has his own conceptual breakfast pizza (tomato, cheese, sausage, bacon, prosciutto, mushroom and a 'drizzle' of egg) or you can indulge in a flaky 'donut' pizza for dessert. There's also a range of non-pizza options like the three-meat pasta with pork, veal and chicken.

Thankfully for those who need a bit of Dutch courage before heading out to the Groove Garden, the bar is fully licensed. Though you might just prefer a beer before checking out the clubhouse. Kiss Pizza reveals itself as a bit of a slapdash establishment, but it's got a big heart. And there's nothing like supporting a local radio station to ensure it survives in this big, bad world.

LIOR OPAT

> ### MIXED BAG

Victoria Park, 274A Johnston St, Abbotsford
(03) 9419 3533
www.kisspizza.com.au
Open Tues–Thurs 8am–10pm, Fri–Sat 8am–late, Sun 4–10pm
(delivery and pick-up only)

See also **map 1 I1**

THE RED TRIANGLE

RACK 'EM UP

The Red Triangle's pool room could be the setting of a 1940s gangster flick. It's the kind of place where you wouldn't be surprised to meet characters who share their names with American cities – like Chicago Joe, the Cincinnati Kid or Minnesota Fats.

Up three flights of rickety stairs, The Red Triangle is a cavernous room with low-hanging lamps, tattered couches and a whole lot of green felt. Once your eyes adjust to the light (or lack there of), you may start to wonder how on earth they got the pool tables up here – surely a painful job unless a crane was involved. Smooth jazz and the knock of billiard balls echoes through the room as players busy themselves around their tables.

But where a gangster flick might turn violent, The Red Triangle remains subdued: it's not a licensed venue, which keeps the tables in perfect condition and the riffraff at bay. The milkshakes are so good you won't even want a beer, and the toasted sandwiches are the exact snack you need to keep up your energy over a few hours of pool.

The sinister side of this place is found mostly in the opening hours (it's open until 2am every day), but the atmosphere is friendly and inviting whatever time you come. If you're really keen, ask the staff to teach you some of the finer points of English billiards or snooker and have a go on one of the full-size tables*.

MATT DERODY

> **MIXED BAG**

110 Argyle St, Fitzroy
(03) 9419 7330
www.redtriangle.com.au
Open Mon–Sun 12pm–2am

See also
map 1 G1

'ENCYCLO' TRIVIA
* Full-size tables are 6 feet x 12 feet – twice the measurements of the pool tables you find in pubs.

077

> MIXED BAG

SPELLBOX THE WITCH'S HOUSE

MAGIC DOES HAPPEN

Women used to be hanged just for being *thought* to practise witchcraft, but with the help of time and the musical *Wicked**, people's attitude towards witches have changed. At Spellbox The Witch's House you can discover the world of magic without the fear of being hanged for it.

Look out for the owl and lantern on Little Bourke Street, climb three flights of stairs and open the door to Spellbox The Witch's House – resident witch Danea's spell and herbal dispensary. Inside it's a heady concoction of incense, herbs, oils and flickering candles lighting a purple, crimson and black lair. Here, Danea offers tarot card, tea leaf and coffee cup readings as well as workshops to help you develop your intuition and spirituality. She can also help you cook up a spell. Simply spin the witch's wheel to discover what you need, combine herbs and oil in a mortar and pestle, and place the mixture in a charm pouch for later use. Boney amber promotes friendship, blacksnake is for courage, and frankincense wards off evil spirits.

If you're interested in learning more about this once dark world, clamber up another rickety flight of stairs to the open-air rooftop. A cauldron in the centre of the rooftop creates the haven where you can study the moon's energy, meditate and cast a ritual spell at the end of the night. All events are centered around times of full and half moon, and Danea runs monthly courses in practical magic – which we promise you can practise openly. **MANDY WILDSMITH**

> **MIXED BAG**

Level 2, 387 Lt Bourke St, Melbourne
(03) 9670 2668
www.spellbox.com.au
Open Mon–Sat 11am–6pm

See also
map 1 D4

'ENCYCLO' TRIVIA
* The musical *Wicked* tells the story of Elphaba, the 'real' woman behind the supposed Wicked Witch of the West in *The Wizard of Oz*.

THE BLACK SHEEP OF MELBOURNE'S LITTLE STREETS

Little Lonsdale Street was always destined to have a special place in Melbourne's history – not least because it's the only one that runs in an easterly direction. The black sheep of Melbourne's little streets, by the 1870s Little Lon was full of sly grog shops, whorehouses, poorhouses, and gambling and opium dens – fertile ground for a war between heaven and hell, and for the authors and historians of the future.

At 39 Little Lonsdale Street you'll find the Oddfellows Hotel, now a pizzeria for the suits working in the soaring glass tower above. If you walk straight ahead into 50 Lonsdale Street, you can check out the loot from archaeological digs of the site before the tower was built, including champagne and perfume bottles, oyster shells and coins. There are also fragments of porcelain knick-knacks and children's toys – a reminder that this place was a home as well as what the fire and brimstone evangelists of the time referred to as Melbourne's den of iniquity.

Around the corner from the Oddfellows is a row of tiny one- and two-storey tenements; look up to see how the scale of life has changed in Melbourne since they were built. An interpretation panel gives a glimpse into the lives of the area's locals but for more creative re-imaginings of the area, check out CJ Dennis's verse novel *Songs of a Sentimental Bloke,* about a group of larrikins from the area at the turn of the 20th century, and LM Robinson's *Madame Brussels: This Moral Pandemonium* – the story of the woman dubbed Melbourne's queen of harlotry (and also the name of a great bar at the top of Bourke Street). Several buildings from the period remain around the block, so go for a wander and conjure up your own version of Melbourne's seedy past. **DALE CAMPISI**

> MIXED BAG

39 Lonsdale St, Melbourne

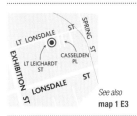

See also
map 1 E3

> MIXED BAG

CRISTINA RE – WHERE A GIRL GOES

PRETTY PAPER, PERFECT PETITS FOURS

Any good Stepford wife will tell you that some occasions call for paper-craft, while others call for petits fours. Cristina Re – Where a Girl Goes brings the two together in unique high tea workshops, where you can learn a little origami or the time-honoured craft of scrapbooking over macaroons, cupcakes, chocolates, tea and coffee, darling.

Whether you want to create party invitations, thank you cards, bonbonnière or paper flowers, Cristina Re knows all the secret techniques and will share them with you over sips of Earl Grey served in vintage fine china. But while the high tea might look sweet and innocent with its candy colours and dainty serving trays, be warned: the sweet treats pack a sugar punch.

Courses start from $30 per person and range from simple card making over pretty pastel cupcakes to the six-hour Brilliant Bride Masterclass. You can get zen with origami or formal with the stationery workshop, and Cristina even caters for the kiddies with craft workshops just for children. All this is to be enjoyed in the dream setting of French chic white lacquer furniture, fabulous chandeliers, and splashes of fleur-de-lis. So gather the ladies for an afternoon in this oasis of feminine delights. Stepford may be a dirty word, but Cristina Re certainly isn't.

KSENIA GOUREEVE

> **MIXED BAG**

Cnr Langridge & Oxford sts,
Collingwood
(03) 9495 6222
www.whereagirlgoes.com
Open Tues–Fri 8.30am–5pm,
Sat 9.30am–4pm

See also
map 1 G3

RELAX MAX

> RELAX MAX

VIGOROUS TRADITIONAL THAI

TIME OUT THAI-STYLE

Melbourne can be a stressful place: unpredictable weather, talking trams and incomprehensible chatter about Aussie Rules. Not to mention getting lost among dumpsters trying to find the latest laneway bar.

But a few moments into a massage at Vigorous Traditional Thai (with two locations in the city and one in West Melbourne), the thing you'll most likely be worrying about is whether your svelte masseuse is actually capable of ripping your arm out of its socket.

The traditional Thai massage is not for the faint-hearted. Or the easily dislocated limb. As it says on their website, you *should* feel sore for a few days afterwards! A full body massage takes place on the floor – all the better for your masseuse to get a good grip and really put their weight into it. But for those who want something a bit softer – and cheaper – there are other options like a neck-and-shoulder only. Even so, the masseuses make good use of their elbows, and show no mercy to knots or tight muscles. But if all this sounds a bit much and you just want to put your feet up, book in a foot massage or reflexology. Judging by the dreamy looks on the customers' faces, these are decidedly more relaxing than vigorous. Just what you need to get refreshed and ready to hit Melbourne's streets once more.   SARAH FRASER

> ### RELAX MAX

391 Bourke St, Melbourne
(03) 9670 5889
www.vigorousthai.com.au
Open Mon–Thurs 10am–10pm
(final massage 9.45pm), Fri 10am–late,
Sat 10.30am–late, Sun 10.30am–8.30pm
(final massage 8.15pm)

See also
map 1 D4

> RELAX MAX

CURLS GONE WILD

The black and grey suits of Little Collins Street wouldn't know what hit them if they stumbled into Wildilocks, a salon which, by the staff's own admission, 'is not yer average'. Owned by Cass Edwards – whose background in fine art is unmistakable – this salon sits at the throbbing heart of Melbourne's alternative scene and takes personal grooming to a whole new, way-out level.

The stylists here are inspired by the melodrama of sub-cultures, from the vintage glamour of 1950s pin-up girl Bettie Paige and the horror and romance of Gothic to steampunk and the theatrical, sexy send-up of burlesque. Visitors can expect the whole gamut of crazy; who knows what might happen when hectic visual drama meets personal grooming! Wildilocks also stocks all the accessories, jewellery and clothes you'll need to complete your new look.

A heady mix of undercuts, extreme asymmetry and wild colours are par for the course, and the stylists themselves are walking canvasses of their own and each other's art. Try painstakingly crafted, chemical-free organic dreadlocks or synthetic, hand-dyed, woollen hair extensions. The possibilities here are limited only by the customer's and stylist's combined capacity for weird.

Wildilocks is an Aladdin's cave of offbeat creative revelry – if Aladdin wore 8-inch stacked boots and a bullet-encased belt, carried a hand grenade change purse and sported a rainbow mohawk! **JENNI KAUPPI**

> ### > RELAX MAX

Level 1, 382 Little Collins St,
Melbourne (enter via McKillop St)
(03) 9642 3384
www.wildilocks.com
Open Tues–Wed 10am–5pm,
Thurs–Fri 10am–7pm, Sat 10am–5pm

See also
map 1 D4

> RELAX MAX

BEAUTIFY ME

Other than tweezing or waxing, I've never been aware of any other options for shaping my eyebrows. But the Indian beautician tells me that she can improve the shape of my eyebrows and accentuate my eyes without any unnecessary damage to my skin. I spy cotton thread on the table and ask what it's for. 'Threading', she tells me. 'You haven't heard of it?'

In the heart of Carlisle Street, eclectic salon Sens' Amore is a melting pot of beauty culture. As well as manicures, pedicures, facials, waxing, and lash and brow tinting, the salon also offers African massage, Jamaican hairstyling, Indian henna tattoos, sheital* (wig) maintenance and threading – the ancient Middle Eastern technique of removing hair with a mini cotton lasso held between the beautician's fingers and their teeth.

You can get your dreadlocks done on a Sunday, but be sure to channel your inner Rasta because it takes most of the day. And if your sheital needs care Sens' Amore offers cuts, blow-dries and colour. Henna tattooists can also paint you up like an Indian bride, without you having to go to the trouble of becoming one. I choose a simple bracelet to adorn my wrist.

With my newly shaped eyebrows and decorated arm perched on the edge of the sofa waiting for the henna to dry, I feel feline. I overhear another client: 'I just don't know how you do it Halli', she sighs. 'That was just incredible.' The salon's owner and top masseur, Halli, combines Western and Eastern techniques of aromatherapy, deep tissue and therapeutic massage with traditional African practices. I watch the customer float out the door and say to Halli, 'I'll book in for whatever she just had.' **LIOR OPAT**

> RELAX MAX

239 Carlisle St, Balaclava
(03) 9527 5877
www.sensamore.com.au
Open Mon–Wed 10.30am–7pm,
Thurs–Sat 10.30am–7.30pm,
Sun by appointment only

See also
map 3 C4

'ENCYCLO' TRIVIA
* Religious Jewish women cover their own hair with a wig, known as a sheital.

> RELAX MAX

ALL THE KING'S MEN: GENTLEMENS HAIRCUTTERS

MAKING MEN MORE ATTRACTIVE THE OLD-FASHIONED WAY

Some men like fauxhawks. Others like their mullets manicured. Still others like an asymmetrical man-bob, but you won't find them at All the Kings Men. This gentleman's haircutter, in what sometimes feels like the city's secret suburb, is no pretentious clipping salon for Melbourne metrosexuals.

All the Kings Men caters only to your fundamental follicular requirements. Scissor cut or buzz cut? The choice is yours. And what a delightfully simple decision it is to make.

No appointments are necessary: simply show up when you need to clean up. Wait your turn on the wooden bench seat (never more than 10 minutes) where there are underground magazines at hand and many a guitar solo on the stereo to keep you entertained. When your name is called, let the barbers get down to the serious business of expert haircutting and male grooming reminiscent of another era, including classic cutthroat razors. There's not a gel or mousse in sight, and you won't have products foisted upon you to maintain that salon-styled look at home.

MICHAEL BRADY

> ## > RELAX MAX

16 Errol St, North Melbourne
(03) 9328 5599
longlivetheking.com.au
Open Tues–Wed 9am–6pm,
Thurs–Fri 9am–7pm, Sat 9am–4pm

See also
map 1 B2

> RELAX MAX

YAN BEAUTY CHINESE MASSAGE

HEAD, SHOULDERS, KNEES AND TOES

There's a scene in *Kill Bill* when Uma Thurman's character, The Bride, awakens from a coma and struggles to get her paralysed feet moving. And even though I'm not a kung fu expert or a ruthless, knife-wielding assassin, I feel for The Bride, I really do. Because this is exactly how my feet feel after a few hours in heels: completely devoid of life.

If only The Bride had known about Yan Beauty Chinese Massage. Here, in a peaceful massage studio two floors above bustling Swanston Street, I heal my aching tootsies with a herbal foot spa and reflexology treatment. After a blissful soak in hot water infused with Chinese herbs and rose petals, a specially trained and qualified masseuse prods, rubs, kneads and knuckles my feet into weapons of dance floor destruction.

At around a dollar a minute, it's serious value. And feet aren't all the ninja-fingered crew at Yan Beauty do: tack a nerve-tingling treatment for head, legs or back onto your time, go completely AWOL with a 1-hour-long full body or hot stone massage, or keep it short and sweet with a neck or head massage for around $5–$10. In fact, there are more massage options here than there are combination dinners in Box Hill*. Walk-ins are welcome, but if you don't have time to wait, you'd best book ahead.

But back to my feet. After jumping, giggling and grimacing my way through 50 minutes of eye-popping, organ-stimulating reflexology (which concludes with a hot towel wrap and calf rub), I don't walk out of Yan Beauty – I float. Me and my heels are ready to show The Bride how to really cut a rug.

VANESSA MURRAY

> **RELAX MAX**

2/149 Swanston St, Melbourne
(03) 9671 3688 or (03) 9005 3688
Open Mon–Sun 10am–8pm

See also
map 1 D4

'ENCYCLO' TRIVIA
* A multicultural suburb 14 km east of Melbourne, Box Hill is renowned for its Asian restaurants and takeaways.

MY OWN HIT THE STREETS DISCOVERIES